The Secret
of
Eln-Ketaar

Stuart J. Whitmore

This story is a work of fiction. Although originally inspired by a true story, all characters, places, and events in this story are entirely fictional and not intended to directly or indirectly depict or represent any real person, event, or location.

Crenel Books
PO Box 33
Sumner WA 98390

ISBN: 978-0-9977780-8-3

In Memory of Ruth

Contents

Chapter One

Nirevella smiled down at her son. Gonterill sat on his straw bed, playing with two of his older sister's simple wood and straw dolls. Faint hunger pangs urged her back to work, and her gaze shifted to the small pile of firewood beside the hearth.

"Malpiek," she said to her husband, "Gisealia is not yet back with more firewood. That girl, she is too easily distracted by her friends. It is late and dark, and the wind is getting stronger. You might need to find her and give her a good scolding about delaying our dinner."

Malpiek nodded without looking up from the knife he was sharpening. "I will go in a moment, when I am done with this. She has been told before not to tarry so much. Perhaps a switch against her backside will be necessary to restore her focus on her duties."

"Do not be too harsh," Nirevella said gently. "She

1

will soon be a young woman, and she also must hone her social skills with her peers."

"A young woman," Malpiek said with a soft snort, "still must attend to her duties, especially when others are relying on her. As for her peers, I hope she is not speaking with Rundarral again. That boy needs to stay away from our daughter, he is much too old to be drawing her attention."

The corners of his wife's mouth turned down. "Indeed, and they both should be very well aware of our thoughts on the matter by now."

"Well," Malpiek said, setting down the knife, "I suppose this will suffice for now. I shall seek out our errant daughter."

"Take your cloak," Nirevella suggested. "I expect rain will reach us soon."

A smile eased Malpiek's features. "Ever the worrier, my love."

She laughed lightly. "That is *my* duty."

He donned his cloak before giving her a quick kiss and heading out into the cold. Their small cottage stood on the north end of Seyelthe, a cozy hamlet perched on a wedge of land that jutted into a large lake. Dense forest surrounded the village as well as the lake, and on the far side of the lake stood tall forested hills where Malpiek and other men of the village often found good hunting.

"Malpiek!" a friendly male voice on his right caught his attention. "Did you see that beast of a fish Varrel caught today?"

Malpiek looked over at his neighbor, whose jovial grin was always a welcome sight. "No, Teslarkin," he said, "I did not. Quite big, I take it?"

"Oh, indeed!" Teslarkin said with a laugh. "It must have been the great-grandfather of every fish of its kind in the lake!"

"Lucky for Varrel and his family," Malpiek said. "Say, have you seen Gisealia? She was only to be gone for a short while collecting firewood, but once again appears to be dawdling, I suspect chatting with her friends instead of working."

A slight frown darkened Teslarkin's face. "I did see her leave your home," he said, "but it looked to me as though she went straight toward the forest. I did not see any of her friends with her. I hope nothing is amiss."

"I see," Malpiek said, with only a slight hint of concern in his voice. "Well, I expect she is fine. She may have found some other thing of interest to take her mind off of her chore. If you are confident that she went straight into the woods, I will head that way myself and see if I can find her. If you see her here in the village, please tell her to go home and stay there until I return."

"I will," Teslarkin agreed with a nod.

Malpiek turned toward a path that would take him into the forest the same way that he assumed his daughter would have gone, since it was the most direct route. Gisealia had been told where to find some thick limbs that had been cut and stacked, so Malpiek strode in that direction first. The more he thought about how long she had been gone, with the weather growing worse, the longer and quicker his strides became.

"Gisealia!" he called out when he reached the first of the trees. "Gisealia!"

There was no answer, and he did not slow his pace. When he reached the pile of cut limbs and saw that none had been taken, his face darkened more. He looked about and called her name repeatedly, but he received no reply. Unsure at first whether to continue looking for her in the forest or return to the village, he decided it would be best to look nearby before returning to the village to see if she was visiting with her friends.

"Gisealia!" he yelled again as he followed the trail deeper into the forest. "Where are you, girl? Gisealia!"

He was about to turn back toward the village when a bit of color in the forest caught his eye. He peered at it a moment before pushing through the underbrush to see what it was. It only took him a few moments to reach Gisealia, who lay curled up on the ground.

"Gisealia!" Malpiek cried out when he saw her. "What is wrong?"

His daughter did not move or respond. He quickly crouched down beside her. A feeling of cold ran down his back when he saw her face. Her eyes were open, but she stared forward as if unaware of herself or her surroundings. One arm was twitching as if possessed, and Malpiek found himself staring at it with dread.

"I must get you home. I must get you back," he said as he picked up his daughter. "I do not understand what has become of you, but I shall summon a healer."

That she still felt warm in his arms eased his worries slightly, but he did not take great solace in it. After pushing his way through the undergrowth to the path, he turned and sprinted back toward his cottage.

"Nirevella!" he cried out. "Nirevella! There is something wrong with Gisealia!"

Teslarkin stepped out of his cottage as Malpiek hurried by. "Is there anything I can do to help?"

"Send for Mishreane, please!" Malpiek said without looking at his neighbor. "Have her come right away!"

"I will seek her myself," Teslarkin said, quickly closing his door behind him. "I believe she is down by the water."

Malpiek paid no further attention to his neighbor as Nirevella came out of their home with a panicked expression. They hurried inside, with Nirevella slamming the door against the cold as Malpiek moved to lay Gisealia on her bed.

"What is wrong with her?" Nirevella asked, rushing to her husband's side.

He shook his head. "I cannot even guess," he admitted as he looked down at his daughter. "Teslarkin told me she had gone straight to the forest, so I went straight there as well. When I saw that she had not touched the wood we stacked before, I looked further into the forest. I nearly missed her. She was off the trail. I was about to head back to look for her within the village. When I found her, she was on the ground just as she is now. Staring into nothing, one arm twitching."

"What are we to do?"

Malpiek gave a weak shrug. "Again, I cannot even guess. Teslarkin is looking for Mishreane right now at my request. Her healing skills are great, she will know what to do. At least Gisealia is safe now, where no wild beast or malicious person can harm her. We can keep her warm, and perhaps get some food into her. I... I don't want to leave, but we also need wood for the fire so that you can prepare our dinner." He sighed heavily. "I will return as soon as I can."

Nirevella grabbed his arm. "Must you? I am afraid, I do not want you to leave. Perhaps we can get by with what we have here now?"

He looked past her to see how much wood was available. "No, my love," he said with a soft shake of his head, "that will only leave us with half-cooked food. I will hurry and-"

"Aah!" Gisealia interrupted her father loudly as her back arched. "No! Make it..." Her voice faded as her body went limp again, save for the arm that still twitched for no apparent reason.

"Oh!" Nirevella cried out, tears sparkling in her eyes. "This is so terrible. I wish Mishreane was here now. Please don't leave yet, Malpiek. I can prepare food that requires less wood, or we can simply have bread and cheese, we need not make a hot meal. I cannot bear to have you gone. And... I..."

Malpiek looked at his wife. "What is it?"

She turned and sobbed into his shoulder. "I... I hate to say this. I hate myself for even speaking these words! Malpiek... she is scaring me. I am afraid for her, but... I am also afraid for us. What if... what if a demon possesses her? What if she attacks us? Perhaps... perhaps I should take Gonterill to a neighbor's for safety."

"No," Malpiek said, stroking her hair, "I don't think it is anything like that. We need not fear her. I trust that you and Gonterill will be safe."

"But... we don't know, you said so yourself," she pointed out. "What if..."

He shook his head again as he held her tight. "Ease your mind, my love. We are safe from her. We just need her to be safe as well, from whatever afflicts her."

A knock at their door startled them. Malpiek eased away from his wife and strode to the door. When he opened it, he found Teslarkin standing with Mishreane. The old woman pushed forward through the door without hesitation and moved promptly to rest on one knee at Gisealia's side. Teslarkin stepped in after a nod from Malpiek, who closed the door promptly.

The healer put her hands on the girl's forehead before pressing her fingers against the wrist that lay still. After a moment, she bent forward to put one ear on Gisealia's chest. Sighing, she slowly got to her feet and turned to look at Nirevella.

"I cannot be certain," she said, her voice rough with age. "It reminds me of something I saw a very long time ago, before you were born. If it is the same, I can do nothing for her. We need Kanzlar."

"Kanzlar," Malpiek said with a frown. "Must we seek such help? I am not sure we have enough coin, and I have heard he rarely accepts anything in barter."

Mishreane turned to look at him. "This is serious and urgent," she said. "I did not speak casually. We *need* Kanzlar. Go to him at once, or have someone go in your stead."

"I can go," Teslarkin said from where he stood by the door.

"I will owe you many favors, friend," Malpiek said. "Thank you."

9

Teslarkin shook his head as he opened the door. "No favors, it is the right thing to do."

As he heard his neighbor's running footsteps fade, Malpiek turned back to the healer. "I need wood for our fire. Can you stay with Nirevella? We have some stacked nearby, it won't take me long."

Mishreane regarded him silently for a moment before giving a short nod. "Be quick."

He met his wife's worried gaze for a moment and then turned to leave. Once outside he found that the rain had started but it was still light. He jogged to the stack of wood under a large tree in the forest, filled his arms, and then strode quickly back to his cottage. After dropping the wood by the door, he returned for more. When he returned with his third armload, with the rain coming down harder, he saw Teslarkin and Kanzlar approaching in the distance. By the time he had moved the firewood inside, the two men had reached his door.

"Please, come in," Malpiek said, giving a quick bow to Kanzlar. "I am sorry to ask you to come out in this weather."

"We have little coin," Nirevella said softly, "but we are willing to barter if there is anything of ours that you would value, or labor that you would like done. We... have never asked for you to use your powers for us, so we don't know..." Her voice trailed off and she looked to her husband with tears in her eyes. He moved to her side to comfort her.

"I'm sure we can arrange something," Kanzlar muttered, sounding annoyed as he pushed back the large hood of his dark cloak to reveal a deeply lined face and flowing white hair.

He moved across the room and stood looking down at Gisealia, who remained still and quiet with no apparent awareness of what was happening. He hummed softly in thought as he watched the twitching arm. Slowly shaking his head, he turned to look at Mishreane.

"No payment will be necessary," he said, his eyes still on the healer. "You did the right thing by sending for me."

"What is wrong with her?" Malpiek asked urgently. "How can you know already? You've only been here a short time, and you have done nothing! And... why is payment unnecessary?"

Kanzlar turned to look Gisealia's parents, his expression grim. "In another circumstance, it would offend me that you would question me so. In this case, I understand. It is your child, and this is nothing like you have seen before. You will not like what I tell you, and I wish I could tell you almost anything else. You know that Mishreane cannot heal her, but neither can I. There is nothing I can do for your daughter, but that is not the worst of it."

"What?" Nirevella cried. "What could be worse than not healing her?"

A sudden sob from Gonterill interrupted them. Seeming to pick up on the tensions in the room, the young boy ran to his mother and clung to one of her legs. She instinctively stroked his hair to calm him, but her eyes never left the wizard standing by her daughter.

"Gisealia has a rare... condition. It is one I have heard of and have been trained to look for," Kanzlar said. "You will not be able to tend to her needs, and at the same time she is a danger to you. Indeed, she is a danger to you, your son, and to the entire village."

Nirevella backed a step away from her daughter's bed, apparently without realizing it.

"A danger?" she asked, her voice full of fear and wonder as she looked from the wizard to her daughter and back again. "She puts the whole village at risk?"

Kanzlar nodded gravely. "We must move her

away immediately," he said. "There is a special place for children like her, where they ensure the children have what they need, while preventing them from harming anyone else. Gisealia must go there in all haste. For her sake, and for yours. And ours."

"Take her away?" Malpiek demanded. "Where is this place?"

"It is far from here," Kanzlar said. "The exact location is kept a secret, for their protection. You can see how vulnerable they are. I will arrange the transportation myself, for my powers can speed her journey."

"How long must she stay?" Nirevella asked. "When will she come back to us?"

Kanzlar sighed. "Most children do not recover from this," he replied. "In fact, I do not know of any who have. When you say goodbye to her, you should understand that it will be the last time you see her. I am sorry. I truly wish I could tell you better news."

"How can this be?" Malpiek said, his voice becoming shrill. "We will never see our daughter again?"

"No," the old wizard confirmed. "Almost certainly not. I suppose there is a faint possibility, but I do not think it is wise to raise your hopes at all. She will be cared for, and she will be kept safe. For now, it is best if you have just one person here in the cottage with her. Malpiek, I suggest that it be you, to keep your wife and son as safe as possible in the circumstances."

"No, this cannot be true..." Malpiek said softly, his voice fading as he looked at his daughter.

Nirevella turned to him. "It is as I said," she said accusingly. "She *is* a danger. You told me she could not be, but she is!"

"He couldn't have known, dear," Mishreane spoke up. "Come, let us find a place where you and Gonterill can stay while Kanzlar makes arrangements. I will make sure you have a chance to see your daughter one more time before she leaves. You will have your chance to say goodbye to Gisealia. Come, dear."

Malpiek watched as the healer led his wife and son out of their cottage. He then looked to Gisealia, who lay still and quiet.

"How did this happen?" he finally asked without looking away from her.

Kanzlar shook his head. "We do not know where this sickness comes from. It is rare. It simply... appears, in certain children, often around this age. I will leave you now with her, for I must arrange for her travel. I must send word ahead, so that her new home knows to expect her."

"Can we, or at least I, go with her on her journey there?"

"No. I am sorry," the wizard said. "You must remain here." He turned toward the door but stopped before opening it. He looked back at Malpiek. "If she comes out of this stupor, keep her here. You must not allow her to wander free! For her safety and that of others, you must keep her here, no matter what she might say. I'm sorry, Malpiek. I know this is difficult."

Malpiek looked to the wizard, his expression hard. "Did you have children, Kanzlar?"

Without answering, the wizard turned and left, closing the door firmly. Malpiek stared at the closed door for a moment and then turned back to Gisealia.

"My dear, sweet daughter," he said softly as he gently brushed a stray lock of her red hair away from her face. "I have failed you, and I do not even know how."

Chapter Two

The speed of the preparations for Gisealia's removal from the village surprised Malpiek. It seemed the wizard had been out of the cottage for only a few moments when he returned, his cloak thoroughly wet, to announce that everything was ready. Only the heavier rain and the empty feeling in Malpiek's stomach from not having eaten dinner confirmed for him that more time had passed than he realized while he waited with his silent and motionless daughter.

"Bring her outside, Malpiek," Kanzlar said with a note of sternness. "There is a carriage and horse ready to take her beyond the north edge of the lake. From there she will transfer to a different mode of transportation to take her across the land more quickly and securely to her new home."

Malpiek looked at the wizard but did not yet move to pick up Gisealia. "Will we be able to write to her at least? Can we send a missive to this home she will be in?"

Kanzlar shrugged. "I do not know," he said. "I believe it will not be possible. Even if they allow it, I am not sure that she will ever be able to understand what you try to tell her. I will inquire, however, if you wish."

"I do."

"Very well," the wizard agreed. "Come, let us not keep the others waiting. Your wife and Mishreanc are out in the rain."

Malpiek looked away quickly as his eyes stung with tears. He gently lifted Gisealia from her bed and kept his face down as he carried her toward the door.

"Gonterill is not here to say goodbye to his sister?" he asked before he reached the door.

"He is so young," Kanzlar answered. "We thought it best if he stay indoors. I do not believe either he or Gisealia would gain from his participation in this sad event."

Malpiek scowled darkly but said no more as he stepped out into the rain. He hunched over Gisealia to keep as much rain from her as possible. True to the wizard's words, he found a simple carriage waiting outside his family's cottage. A moment later, he recognized it as a rarely-used vehicle belonging to one of the wealthier villagers on the other side of Seyelthe. He saw his wife and the healer standing near the open door of the carriage, but the driver was cloaked and hooded, and Malpiek could not tell who it was.

"We have a blanket on the floor of the carriage," Mishreane said as Malpiek reached the carriage. "Lay her gently on that."

He paused to kiss his daughter's forehead. Nirevella also stepped up to kiss Gisealia's forehead, although she seemed hesitant to be so close. With tears streaming down his cheeks, Malpiek placed his daughter on the coarse blanket that lay on the floor of the carriage.

"It is painful," Mishreane said, placing one hand gently on his arm when he finally stood straight again, "but it is for the best."

"She'll be cared for well," Kanzlar said as he closed the carriage door. "Driver, you may proceed."

At a mild prompt from the driver, the horse moved forward. The four adults standing in the rain watched the carriage roll away, but Kanzlar and Mishreane took their leave before it was out of sight. When Malpiek and Nirevella could no longer see it, they turned to each other and collapsed into each other's arms, crying hard.

"I will go get Gonterill," Nirevella finally said as their embrace ended. "Go in and dry off."

Malpiek nodded. "I will build up the fire. This will be a dark and cold night regardless, but we might as well have what heat and light we can."

Gisealia slowly opened her eyes. As her vision cleared and her thoughts followed, panic raced through her. There was no question that she was not at home, nothing looked or felt familiar. She tried to sit up from the strange bed on which she found herself, but coarse leather straps bound her arms and ankles.

"So, you are finally awake," an unfamiliar woman's voice said from her left.

She looked over to the source of the voice. An old woman in a simple gray dress sat on an equally simple wooden stool. The woman's face was stern and lined with deep wrinkles, and her thinning hair was almost pure white with just a hint of gray.

"Wh-where am I?" Gisealia asked, stammering in fear.

The woman abruptly lifted up a thin willow

switch and brought it down hard on Gisealia's arm. "Where am I, *madam*?" she said sternly. "You will address your elders with *respect* here. I don't care what the custom was wherever you came from. You are now in Eln-Ketaar. In Eln-Ketaar, children have *manners*."

"What is El-Eln-Ketaar, m-madam?" Gisealia forced out the words, not allowing herself to look at her arm to see if the welt she expected to see was already visible.

"Eln-Ketaar is a home for girls like you," the woman said. "I came to Eln-Ketaar as a young girl and I have never left. You have much to learn here, but you will have plenty of time, because you will never leave either."

"N-n-never l-leave? M-madam?"

The woman twitched the willow branch but did not strike Gisealia with it. "You have an illness," she stated flatly. "It is not one that has a cure. You are a danger to others, as am I. We all are. If Eln-Ketaar did not give us a home, we would certainly be slain. We must always be grateful that we are allowed to live, and we show our gratitude through hard work."

Gisealia looked down at the straps holding her arms. "What work, madam?" she asked quietly.

"That depends," the woman answered. "If you behave, you will be working in textiles. If you are disobedient, disrespectful, or try to run away, you will be working in the mine. Most girls end up in the mine at least once. The smart ones realize they need to avoid being sent there again. Were you the type to obey your parents?"

"Yes, madam."

The woman gave a soft sniff of amusement. "All the new girls say so."

The sound of a door opening echoed faintly in the room. The old woman stood as rapidly as she could, although Gisealia could see that her age slowed her. The woman bowed stiffly to the newcomer, but Gisealia could neither move nor see who had arrived.

"Is the new one ready?" a man's voice asked.

"Almost, sir," the woman said as she stood straight again. "She only woke a few moments ago. I have started to explain what is expected of her."

"Does she seem safe?" the man asked, his tone dour.

"Yes, sir," the woman answered. "She is not combative, just confused, as new ones always are."

Gisealia heard a sigh that sounded annoyed. "Very well, get her up, clean, and fed. The thin broth we've been feeding her while she slept won't give her sufficient energy for today's work, even though she is starting late. The leftovers from the midday meal may not have been disposed of yet. Get her on the floor as quickly as you can."

"Yes, sir."

A moment later, Gisealia heard the door close. The woman turned back to face her and eased herself back down onto the stool.

"We will start you on a spinning wheel," she said. "Have you used one before?"

"No, madam."

The woman shrugged. "We will teach you. It is simple enough. If you prove to be skilled and intelligent enough, we will move you up in the production process. We mainly produce unfinished textiles that are shipped away to those who make them into finished products. This is how we pay for our home, our food, and our safety. Occasionally we sew clothing as well, mostly for our own use, although from time to time women who are particularly skilled at sewing will make clothing according to specifications we receive from buyers. To augment our earnings, we also work a copper mine. It does not produce much, though, and it is used mostly for discipline. Do you have any questions so far?"

"No, madam."

"Good," the woman said with a frown. "Although the main rule is that you are generally expected to remain quiet and well-behaved at all times, we also have some specific rules. First, you must stay within Eln-Ketaar at all times. There is no running within the building unless there is a life-threatening emergency such as a fire. There is absolutely no talking while working, unless the talk is specifically about work. You are allowed to converse quietly with those seated near you at the same table during meals, but rowdy behavior and loud voices will not be tolerated.

"You will see few men here. You will not speak to them unless they address you. If they speak to you, you will only respond to their questions. You are not to volunteer anything. They are the masters of Eln-Ketaar and they do not have time for idle chat or silly questions.

"The room you are in now is only for newcomers. You will be assigned a bed in the barracks tonight. You will go to bed at the same time as everyone else, the lights will be turned out at the same time every night, and you will not rise during the night. You will get up when everyone else rises, and all meals are taken together. No food may be eaten outside of meal times or away from tables in the dining hall.

"The final rule is perhaps the most important. If, at any time, you see another resident showing any signs of their illness, you must raise an alarm immediately. The masters of Eln-Ketaar use their powers to keep our sickness under control, but on rare occasion a girl with a particularly bad case may need extra attention. Do you have any questions?"

"N-no, madam."

"Good," the woman said again. "Before I release you from the straps, which we use for your protection as well as ours, I will tell you that the masters of Eln-Ketaar are always available and frequently observing us whether we can see them or not. We may use the privy and bathe out of their sight, but we should not expect to not be seen otherwise. I tell you this in case you are inclined to attack me, or run away, or do some other foolish thing. The masters are powerful, and there are worse punishments than working the mines."

"Yes, madam."

The woman stood again and began removing the leather straps. Gisealia sat up slowly, not wanting to alarm the woman. Her mind whirled with more questions, despite her claim to not have any, but she didn't think the woman would take the time to ease her confusion. The older woman had clearly been focused on what was expected of Gisealia, and other questions would have to wait or remain unanswered. She stood and looked down at the dress she now wore, which was almost identical to the one worn by the old woman, although hers was wrinkled while the woman's was neatly pressed.

"This way," the woman said once Gisealia was on her feet.

After allowing a brief bath in cool water and giving Gisealia a fresh dress, the old woman led her through the large stone building to a room full of long wooden tables with wood benches. She commanded Gisealia to sit before disappearing through a door. She returned with a metal plate bearing simple food and a metal cup containing only water. Gisealia ate quickly under the dismal gaze of the older woman.

"Time for work," the woman said as soon as Gisealia was done. "Leave those. A girl on kitchen duty will pick them up. We rotate duties, of course, so eventually you will do kitchen duty too, and many other things. Follow me."

Gisealia followed the woman out of the dining hall

and along a confusing route of passageways. Eventually they reached a long, wide room with a high ceiling. There were no windows low on the walls, but light shone through windows near the top. More light came from lanterns mounted on the walls and on the pillars that held up the ceiling. Gisealia saw dozens of girls and women of all ages sitting at spinning wheels, while a few others moved about distributing supplies and collecting finished work. Everyone wore dresses the same as hers. Nobody spoke, and nobody looked to the door to see who had entered.

"Nikaijila," the old woman said as she led Gisealia to one side, "this is Gisealia. She doesn't know how to spin. You will teach her. *No idle chatter.* I know how your mouth runs. I will be paying attention."

"Yes, madam," Nikaijila answered.

Gisealia found herself staring at the younger girl. She had never seen someone with such dark skin before. The people of her village all had light-colored skin, and most had straight hair that was either red like hers or a shade of yellow. Nikaijila's hair looked to be completely black, and her tight curls stayed close to her head.

As Nikaijila stood up, she caught Gisealia's stare

and smirked with amusement. "Sit here," she instructed. "You've never spun at all, even by hand?"

"No," Gisealia answered with a quick shake of her head.

She quickly glanced at the old woman before sitting on the stool at the spinning wheel. The old woman simply stood and watched.

"It is not hard to learn," Nikaijila said confidently.

True to what she had been told, Gisealia found that she picked up the task quickly. When it was clear that she could be productive on her own, the old woman reassigned Nikaijila to be a runner, gathering and distributing materials for those working on the wheels. Gisealia didn't see much more of that woman for the rest of the day, but there were other older women who moved about supervising the work. It was clear that she was expected to stay focused on her work, so she made no effort to look around at the other workers in the room. True to what the first woman she had met had said, there was very little talking and all of it was strictly about the work they were doing.

Despite her intent to not be distracted from her work, Gisealia jumped slightly in surprise when she heard a sharp sound. Instinctively she looked toward it and saw that one of the women supervising the work had struck a girl across the shoulders with a willow switch.

"Pay attention!" the supervisor snapped. "We do not need your mistakes to cause complaints from our buyers." The woman then turned to Gisealia, apparently having noticed that she was looking. "Get back to work! The only thing you should be looking at is the wheel before you!"

Gisealia promptly returned to her work, feeling the sting of tears of embarrassment. She was sure that her face was turning red. Whenever her thoughts turned to her family and her longing to be back in her home village, she shoved those thoughts aside to focus on what she was doing. She had no intention of being the next recipient of the switch.

In the evening, after the light coming from the upper windows had faded, a harsh bell sounded from somewhere in the room. In the corner of her eye, Gisealia saw the other women standing up, so she got to her feet too. She was glad to be able to stop working finally, but she wasn't sure what to expect next. Her heart started to race when it looked like one of the supervisors was approaching her, but the stern-looking woman passed by and stood for a moment by the door.

"Come," she said simply before stepping out of the room.

The workers quietly moved to follow her, so Gisealia moved to join in, all the while feeling unsure that she was doing the right thing. As they moved through the building, she suddenly felt the jab of an elbow in one arm. She looked in that direction and saw Nikaijila had moved up to walk next to her. The younger girl had a smirk on her face, although she kept her eyes forward. Taking that as a cue, Gisealia quickly shifted her gaze toward the front as well.

The supervisor in the lead brought them to the dining hall where Gisealia had eaten before starting work. Once they were inside the hall, the girls and women moved a little less formally, but there was still little talking as they formed a line for food. Gisealia stayed with Nikaijila and followed her example, picking up a battered metal plate from a stack and moving forward to get her ration. When she received her food from one of the women doling it out, she couldn't help but notice how small the portion was, and she hoped it would be enough to fend off her hunger until morning.

"Where are you from?" Nikaijila asked quietly

once they were seated next to each other.

"It's a small village called Seyelthe. You probably haven't heard of it," Gisealia answered before taking a bite of her dinner.

Nikaijila grinned. "You're right. Never heard of it. I'm from a small island called Teyes-takan. And yes, I saw your look, just like I've seen it from all the others. All of us on the island have skin this dark. I had never been off the island, never seen pale skin like yours, until I woke up here."

Gisealia's eyebrows went up. "I thought I was shocked and scared when I woke up here," she said after swallowing. "You must have been terrified."

"I was–" Nikaijila started to say, but a loud crash behind them cut her off.

Gisealia turned in surprise and saw that a girl who looked a few years older than her had fallen, dropping her plate and cup, strewing food and splashing weak juice on the wood floor. The girl looked around with a terrified expression as she tried to collect herself. When one of the older women stormed toward her, the girl suddenly turned and pointed at Gisealia.

"She tripped me!"

The older woman stopped when she reached the girl and turned sharply to face Gisealia.

"Did you trip her?"

"No, madam," Gisealia answered, sounding both scared and offended.

The woman looked at Nikaijila. "Did she trip her?"

"No, madam," Nikaijila answered seriously.

The woman stared at Nikaijila for a moment. "I don't believe *you*," she said with a faint snarl. "Both of you will be in the mine tomorrow."

Nikaijila looked away quickly. Gisealia was not as quick to hide her stunned reaction. The woman's eyes narrowed in a clear challenge, but Gisealia looked down, forced her expression to relax, and turned back to her food.

"Next time, watch your footing better," the woman said to the other girl. "Clean up your mess. You can go without food tonight. Perhaps that will teach you to watch out for obstacles that might appear in front of you."

Gisealia stared at her food while the girl who had fallen worked to clean the food and drink from the floor. Nikaijila nudged her and motioned to her plate, and Gisealia realized there might be some punishment if she did not eat all of her dinner. She forced herself to resume eating despite her sudden lack of hunger.

Chapter Three

After the evening meal, Gisealia was assigned to a different room where she learned how to weave fabrics on a loom. Nikaijila was returned to the spinning wheel room, so the two only saw each other again after the evening shift was done and they were on their way to the barracks. Supervisors led the women and girls in groups to the dormitory wing of the building, and Gisealia was relieved when she was assigned to the same barracks room as Nikaijila. The younger girl was the friendliest face and the only person whose name Gisealia knew, and she hoped they might become friends, if Eln-Ketaar allowed friendship.

In each barracks room there were two rows of wood-frame bunk beds. On each bed was a basic mattress filled with straw, and heavy wool blankets were neatly folded at the foot of each bed. The supervisor who led Gisealia's group into her room showed her which bed she was to use, which was the bottom bunk under a bunk that was missing its mattress. The woman rattled off information that Gisealia would need to know and then stalked away without asking if she had any questions.

Nikaijila's bunk was further down the same row, so Gisealia followed the examples set by the other girls and women around her to prepare for bed, which they did rapidly and with little talk. Once she was finally in bed, she had time to think through the strange and difficult day, and her eyes filled with tears as she thought about her home in Seyelthe. She was tired after a full day of work, but she wondered if her busy mind would let her sleep.

Gisealia awoke suddenly. She didn't remember falling asleep, but there was light coming through high windows she hadn't noticed the night before. The others in the barracks were promptly getting out of bed and getting ready for the day, so she moved quickly to catch up. When a supervisor came in to lead them down for their morning meal, she was as ready as the rest.

As soon as the meal was over, Gisealia and Nikaijila joined a group of girls who were led to the mine entrance. A short covered breezeway stretched from a door of the building to the opening of a dark mine that had been bored into a steep cliff face. The walls of the breezeway had glassless windows along the top to let light and air through, but Gisealia could not see much of the surrounding area other than rugged mountains towering nearby. On the mine end, there was a grated opening in the floor. As she passed by, Gisealia saw that there was a small and sturdy cart parked under the opening.

Her work that day was much harder, and supervisors brought them rations for the midday meal instead of allowing the workers to leave the mine. Despite the harder work, Gisealia found that there was some relief in what was supposed to be a punishment. Talking was still sternly discouraged, but her assignment to take loads of rock out to dump through the grate kept her moving and not constantly under the watchful eye of the supervisors. The work also allowed her mind to wander. She had time to question everything, from how the cart below the grate was moved for emptying, to the nature of the sickness that forced her and the others to be kept within the confines of Eln-Ketaar.

When the day ended and Gisealia lay down on her bed, she did not question whether she would be able to sleep, for she felt exhausted. Still, it felt unusual to awaken the following morning with no recollection of falling asleep and no awareness of any dreams during the night.

She and Nikaijila were allowed to return to textile work, which required more focused thought and offered no time for her mind to wander into questioning what had become of her life. During meals, though, she wondered whether the strange sleep rhythm was just a symptom of her condition or if the masters of Eln-Ketaar did something with their magic to control the women and girls at night.

"Did you have wizards in your village?" Nikaijila asked her one day during an evening meal.

Gisealia nodded. "One. His name was Kanzlar. I rarely saw him, he kept to himself and was not very friendly. People paid for his help sometimes, but he asked high prices."

Nikaijila looked surprised. "That is strange," she commented. "We had none on our island, but there were two on a nearby island. They were very friendly and visited our island frequently. They would be ashamed to take payment for helping someone, and they often entertained us with their magic." She smiled as she looked down at her food. "One sent me up into the air and would not let me down until I sang a silly song as loud as I could. I miss my home."

"I miss mine, too," Gisealia said softly. "I've lost track of how many days I have been here, but it feels like only yesterday that I was playing with Gonterill. That is my little brother."

"Time passes without us noticing here," Nikaijila agreed. "I try to count our sleeps sometimes, but I doubt I have kept accurate count. I wonder if any of the older women have any idea how long they have been here."

Gisealia glanced up at a supervisor as she walked by. She averted her eyes quickly, but it was an interesting question. The prospect of living out her years in Eln-Ketaar was troubling, and it made her curious about what danger she posed to others that was so severe that she would be doomed to such a fate.

Weeks turned to months, and months turned to years. Gisealia knew she was growing because she was given new dresses when she grew out of old ones. She spent most of the time working in textiles, but on occasion she would break some minor rule on purpose just to have a break by working in the mine instead.

A new girl finally arrived and was assigned the bunk over her. Other than quietly telling Gisealia that her name was Feirsallene, the newcomer refused to speak or meet anyone's gaze, so Gisealia did not pressure her. She remembered how difficult it had been to adjust to the dull and sad life at Eln-Ketaar, and she hoped the newcomer would open up eventually.

"Tomorrow it's the mine for both of you!" an old supervisor snapped at Gisealia and Nikaijila.

"Yes, madam," Gisealia said quietly, bowing her head to make sure the woman didn't see any trace of amusement.

"Yes, madam," Nikaijila echoed her.

When the woman was gone, Gisealia resumed eating her evening meal. She avoided looking at Nikaijila, for she knew that either one of them might burst out laughing. The two young women had planned earlier in the day to do something that would send them to the mine, just for a change of pace, and their minor mischief had worked according to plan.

The next morning, Gisealia awoke with the rest of the women and girls in the barracks. She knew she had a hard day of work ahead, for the labor of working in the mine was never easy, but she still looked forward to a break from the dull routine of working in textiles. As she readied herself for the day, she glanced at Feirsallene and noticed that the new girl was simply standing still, looking down at the floor.

"Is all well, Feirsallene?" she asked softly but with a sense of urgency. "You must keep up. You did not like the one time that you worked in the mine before, you don't want to give them reason to send you there again."

Feirsallene looked up slowly. "All is well," she answered, her voice flat. "I will keep up."

Gisealia continued her own preparations but remained aware of Feirsallene too, without watching her directly. She was concerned about the other girl and wondered if the sickness they all shared was somehow affecting her worse. If it was, Gisealia knew she needed to alert a supervisor. After being prompted by her, though, Feirsallene seemed to move through the morning routine normally.

"Feeling strong?" Nikaijila asked Gisealia with a hint of humor when they sat down together for their morning meal.

"Strong enough," Gisealia affirmed with a nod. "Perhaps I shall discover a new vein and make Eln-Ketaar richer than ever before."

Her friend chuckled softly. "I think the rocks you have mined have ended up in your head."

When the meal was over, Gisealia and Nikaijila joined the group of women and girls heading to the mine. Unlike her first experience there, it now seemed routine for Gisealia. She felt mildly disappointed once they were in the mine and she received her first assignment, but she knew her task of taking the rock chips to dump through the grate would only last until midday. She hoped that she and Nikaijila could work together after that.

Gisealia had just started toward the mine entrance with her first load, carrying two buckets of broken rock because other workers had taken the wheeled carts, when a low rumble filled the mine. She looked around fearfully as the ground started to shake. The other workers stopped what they were doing as well. Dust and sand sifted down from the ceiling.

"What do we do?" one of the younger girls cried out, just as the rumbling faded away.

"You get back to work!" one of the supervisors snapped. "It happens from time to time. Ignore it and keep working!"

Gisealia felt uneasy as she set out toward the entrance again. In the time she had been at Eln-Ketaar, nothing like that had happened. The first time she had worked in the mine, her awareness of being underground had only been in the back of her mind because she was fearful of the supervisors. Since then, working in the mine had not seemed particularly dangerous. After the ground quaked, however, she no longer felt as safe, even though no harm was done.

She paused by a side tunnel that she had passed many times before. A supervisor had once told Gisealia that it was an exploratory cut that Eln-Ketaar abandoned when it did not produce enough to continue mining. It was blocked by a small pile of broken rock, and mine workers were instructed that nobody was to enter it. Gisealia rarely noticed it anymore, but this time it somehow caught her attention.

She looked around and saw that she was alone for a moment. She knew there were harsher punishments than just being assigned to work in the mine for a day or a week, and she knew that entering the side tunnel was likely to result in just such a punishment. Yet despite knowing that she should quickly return to her task, she stood at the opening of the tunnel and looked into it.

She couldn't understand why it attracted her attention. It was almost as if she had caught a whiff of an unfamiliar smell, or heard something very faint, or saw a slight movement. Something she couldn't quite grasp felt different. After another look around to make sure nobody would see her, she quickly scrambled over the pile of rocks.

"I will pay for this, I know I will," she whispered softly. "And I'm a fool for thinking it will somehow be worth the risk."

Once past the rubble, Gisealia moved quickly away from the main tunnel so that anyone passing by would not see her. The side tunnel angled down and curved to the left. Before long she was out of sight of the entrance, and she paused to set down her buckets of rock so that she could move more easily. The lights from the main tunnel did not offer much illumination, and she knew she would quickly run out of light entirely.

Gisealia was about to turn back when she couldn't see anymore, but something caught her attention again. She peered into the inky darkness in the direction of whatever it was, but she felt sure that she was only looking at a blank wall. After staring at it for a long moment, she turned away, only to have her attention caught by it again.

"What strange thing is this?" she whispered, her words barely audible even to herself.

When she looked directly at the wall, she could see nothing. Yet when she turned her head, she saw, or felt, something different. It seemed as if tiny orbs, faintly glowing of green, were coming out of the wall, but despite sensing them and even understanding their color, she could not see them directly.

Curious and yet fearful, she reached out to touch the place in the wall from which the orbs seemed to emanate. She felt a thin crack in the stone, and she ran her fingertips along it. A pale green light briefly flickered in the darkness, and Gisealia gasped in surprise.

A sense of energy flowed up through her arm and into her core. Vague images spun in her mind, and her breathing slowed. Her senses seemed amplified, so that she could see her surroundings better, hear the faintest sounds, and even taste the air that she breathed. She knew she should be afraid, but fear did not rise within her.

In the dark tunnel, she saw the faint, shimmering image of an old woman appear. Even then, with a ghostly apparition gazing at her, Gisealia felt no fear. All she could feel was a profound sense of awe.

"I have waited long for one such as you," the woman said.

"Who are you, madam?" Gisealia asked aloud before realizing that perhaps the woman had not actually spoken aloud. "And... what are you, madam, if I may be so bold as to ask?"

The ghostly woman smiled. "You may be so bold, and I am just a woman like you, though with many more years behind me. You need not call me madam, there is no need for formality between us. In fact, formality will simply hamper our efforts to complete the tasks that face us. You may call me Ree."

"Ree?" Gisealia asked. "And if you are just a woman, mada– Ree, then how are you appearing to me so?"

Ree's smile grew. "You have much to learn and I am eager to teach it. Ree, by the way, is short for my real name. Ree is quicker and easier to say, but perhaps in time I will teach you the pronunciation of my full name. What is your name, child? And do I understand correctly that you are in Eln-Ketaar? In the mine?"

"Yes," Gisealia said. "My name is Gisealia."

"That's a pretty name," Ree said. "I look forward to working with you, Gisealia."

"Working, m– Ree?"

Ree nodded. "Not labor like you are doing now, but work of a different nature, and vastly more important than making old men wealthy. But first things first, you must get out of Eln-Ketaar before they detect that you have accessed mana and used magic."

"I... Mana? Used magic? I am confused."

"I will explain when we are together in person," Ree assured her. "You must trust me, you are in danger right now and must escape quickly. Follow my instructions, and we will meet soon."

Gisealia shook her head. "I cannot escape, Ree. They watch us always. I could not reach an outer door before someone stopped me."

Ree nodded again. "Indeed, so you will not use a door. And they are luckily not watching you now, else they would have interfered promptly. Come to me now, I will instruct you how, and we can talk in depth once you are safe."

"I... I can't leave my friend," Gisealia said. "I can't leave her behind if she is in danger."

"She won't be, if she has not used magic," Ree said. "It really is urgent that you leave now, Gisealia. I cannot be sure they won't kill you if they find out what you have done."

"What I... By talking to you?"

"That and more," Ree said. "Please, Gisealia. I can't force you, but you must come to me quickly."

Gisealia shook her head firmly. "I can't, not if there is risk that Nikaijila might be killed if she stumbles upon what I have."

Ree pursed her lips and was silent for a moment. "Very well, I can teach you how to bring your friend with you, but you must understand that this comes at incredible risk to yourself, perhaps even risk of death."

"I am barely living here," Gisealia said with a shrug. "This is no life to preserve. If we can escape, it is worth that risk." She hesitated. "But what of our illness? We are sick, we are a danger to others. That is why we are here. I... I should not leave, I don't know why I thought it would be all right if I escaped."

Ree shook her head sadly. "No," she said with a hint of anger, "you are not sick. You have no illness. You have the ability to wield magic, and that is all."

"That cannot be," Gisealia said. "I know you said that I used it, but women can't actually–"

"Women can," Ree interrupted. "I am using it, right now, which is why you can see me. It is how I detected that someone had finally accessed the mana that I have been trying to pour in that direction for decades. And that act over the years could only have been accomplished by doing the very thing that we are told women can't do. Gisealia, women are not *allowed* to wield magic. It has nothing to do with ability."

"But... all of the women and girls here..."

"Can all wield magic," Ree confirmed. "We must move quickly, Gisealia. This discussion must be delayed for later. If you will not come with me now, then I must instruct you on how to secretly store mana within you, and then I must instruct you in the process that you will use to depart Eln-Ketaar and meet me."

"I am afraid," Gisealia said, realizing that fear had finally found her, but it was for what she faced from the men and supervisors of Eln-Ketaar rather than the strange experiences in the dark mine shaft.

Ree nodded. "That is natural. Now, listen carefully. I will step you through some of what you must do, but some must be done on your own later when you are with your friend."

When she returned to the light shining in from the main tunnel, Gisealia could tell there was a commotion resulting from her apparent disappearance. She ignored the buckets of rock and held back in the darkness to watch as supervisors and workers moved back and forth, with the supervisors barking commands. Ree had eased her through the process of manipulating magic to turn herself invisible, yet she couldn't dismiss the fear of being discovered. Taking a deep breath, she moved forward.

In the main tunnel she had to be wary of colliding with the workers and supervisors. It quickly became apparent that there were many more supervisors than would normally be in the mine, so Gisealia assumed that an alarm had been raised in the main building. She strode quickly down into the mine, hoping her friend was still at work and not taking part in the search.

Gisealia breathed a sigh of relief when she saw Nikaijila swinging a pickaxe with little enthusiasm, looking frequently away from her work to see what was happening. When she was only a few steps away, Gisealia spoke her name in a whisper. Her friend turned around, a wild look in her eyes.

"Nikaijila, trust me," Gisealia whispered as she got closer. "This will be scary, but we must do it."

"You!" a nearby supervisor shouted at Nikaijila. "Stop gawking and get back to work, or you'll get the switch!"

"Trust me," Gisealia hissed urgently as she grasped Nikaijila's arm firmly.

Her friend's eyes grew wide at the sudden touch, and she looked fearfully at the supervisor who was now storming toward her. Gisealia did her best to tune out the approaching danger as she recited the words that Ree had made her memorize. The supervisor was only steps away when Gisealia finished. A heartbeat later, the older woman gave a shout of surprise as Nikaijila disappeared from before her eyes.

Chapter Four

Gisealia stood in a daze. After a moment, she remembered to release her invisibility spell. Nikaijila jumped back in surprise when she suddenly appeared in the sunlit meadow next to her.

"Sorry!" Gisealia said. She shivered and gave her head a shake as if to clear something away. "I am so sorry to startle you, in many ways, Nikaijila."

"Where are we?" her friend demanded. "How did we get here? What are we doing here?"

"We're going to meet someone," Gisealia said. "We're here because we escaped Eln-Ketaar."

"No!" Nikaijila vehemently shook her head. "We *can't* be out of Eln-Ketaar, Gisealia! We're a danger, don't you remember? We were there to keep us safe and to keep others safe from us. Have you forgotten the sickness?"

Gisealia smiled faintly. "I have not forgotten it,"

she said. "I learned today what it is, and it is not a sickness."

"How?" Nikaijila demanded. "How did you learn? How did you bring us here? This makes no sense!"

"Not yet, but it will," Gisealia said, trying to stay calm while feeling excited to finally be out of the dreary confines of Eln-Ketaar. "I will explain while we wait for our guide."

Nikaijila looked around. "Guide?"

Gisealia laughed. "Let me explain!"

Taking a deep breath and noting how nice the morning sun felt on her face, Gisealia explained what had happened in the mine. She couldn't fully describe the magical energy that Ree called mana, but she explained everything else as best she could.

"And so now we wait here?" Nikaijila asked when her friend finished. She looked around. "And we'll magically recognize whatever guide this Ree woman sends to us?"

Gisealia nodded. "She assured me that we would recognize our guide, although she didn't say that it was by magic."

The younger woman shook her head. "We come from very different places," she reminded Gisealia. "The only people we would both recognize are people in Eln-Ketaar."

"I don't think that's what she meant," Gisealia said with a little shrug. "I just... I... Nikaijila, look at that!"

Her friend turned to see what she was pointing at and gasped. Near the edge of the meadow, she saw a pure white unicorn standing proudly by a large tree that stood out from the surrounding forest. The unicorn was clearly looking at them, and after a moment it dipped its head. The gesture was not submissive, but instead it seemed to be an acknowledgment and greeting.

"I think that might be our guide!" Gisealia whispered excitedly.

"I didn't think they were real," Nikaijila replied, her voice full of wonder. "I thought they were just fanciful tales, a story made to make the mainland sound wondrous."

"Should we approach it?" Gisealia asked.

As if in answer, the unicorn dipped its head again. The young women exchanged excited glances and then started to move across the meadow toward the majestic creature. When she felt that she was close enough, Gisealia curtsied and bowed her head slightly, and Nikaijila followed her example.

The unicorn slowly turned and walked toward the forest, glancing back once to make sure the women were following. They followed it into the wood, staying back a respectful distance. After a short distance, they reached a wide, shallow stream. The unicorn paused briefly at the water's edge before trotting through the water to the other side. Once there, it turned back to the women and tilted its head, as if pointing to the water with its horn.

"I'm not sure what it wants us to do," Gisealia admitted as she stepped forward. "I feel like we will be too close to it if we step into the water."

Nikaijila merely shrugged, her eyes on the unicorn. They approached slowly, to make sure the unicorn did not object, but it merely stood and watched. With a glance at her younger friend, Gisealia stepped out carefully into the stream. Her eyes darted down with surprise when her feet did not enter the water but rested on its surface instead with the water continuing to flow underneath.

As soon as Nikaijila stood on the water by her side, the unicorn dipped its head once more. The young women gasped in surprise again as they started moving upstream, their feet not moving and the water flowing unimpeded in the other direction. They looked back at the unicorn just in time to see it disappear into the trees.

"This is strange and scary," Nikaijila admitted. "How do we know when to step off the water?"

A faint grin eased Gisealia's features. "I think we will know, just as we knew to follow the unicorn."

The mysterious magic carried them far along the river, passing through forest and fields toward mountains in the distance. As time passed, Gisealia began to fear that she had been wrong and that perhaps she had missed some sign that it was time to leave the water. She was about to voice her concern as they entered a new stand of trees when their motion slowed to a stop.

"You were right," Nikaijila said with a laugh. "We will know."

"I am relieved," Gisealia said. "I was starting to worry that I had made a mistake."

"No mistake," Ree's voice came from nearby, and a moment later the woman appeared from behind a leafy bush. "It is good to meet you in person! Come, step off the water, my home is nearby." She looked to Nikaijila as the women moved to the stream bank. "You are different. From the islands?"

"Yes, madam," Nikaijila confirmed.

Ree laughed lightly. "Just Ree, not madam," she said. "And if I remember correctly from my discussion earlier with Gisealia, your name is Nikaijila."

"Yes, m– Ree," she said with a grin.

Ree led them along a neatly manicured path toward a large cottage that was surrounded by a tidy fence and a well-tended garden. They went inside without delay, and Gisealia found herself looking around the cozy home with admiration as the old woman poured tea for them.

"It is so nice to have visitors," Ree said with a gentle smile as she produced a tray of sweet cakes. "The three of us have our work cut out for us, I assure you, but we might as well enjoy our time together while it lasts. Please, have a seat, there is so much to discuss."

By nightfall, Gisealia and Nikaijila understood the truth of Eln-Ketaar. They understood that it was a place to collect any girl who showed sensitivity to magic, to keep them controlled so that only men would be allowed to wield it. Ree sat through outbursts of rage, tears of grief, and thoughtful silence as the two younger women came to grips with what had happened to them. She sat by as they experienced a flood of envy at her for not being collected into Eln-Ketaar out of sheer luck, and being equally lucky in finding a dying old wizard who took enough pity on her to teach her how to control her powers.

"Always remember," Ree said as they began to prepare for bed that night, "that your families had no idea what was happening. Do not believe for a moment that they would have sent you away knowing how you would be treated. Eln-Ketaar has stood for a long time, since long before I was born, and there were times when the work that was done there was much less pleasant than textiles and mining. For countless years, the secret has been held closely. Do not blame your parents for not knowing what very few in the land know."

Gisealia stood by the bed the older woman had prepared for her. "The wizards, though," she said darkly. "Kanzlar. In my village. He knew."

Ree shrugged at first, and then nodded slowly. "He probably has some idea, but I doubt he knows the full truth. He knew that you could wield magic, this much I think cannot be denied. Whether he knew what you would actually face at Eln-Ketaar, other than having your powers subdued, we can only guess."

"The wizards knew that any girl who showed the signs would be sent there," Nikaijila said, frowning, "while boys who showed the signs would be treated as special and promptly taught how to control their powers. It leaves a hole in my heart to know that the wizards I knew, who always seemed so pure and good and fun, knew they were taking part in this fraud."

Ree nodded again. "It does hurt, I understand that. But remember, they might know very little of the truth. They might actually believe that you are a danger, which, I suppose, any boy or girl who doesn't know how to control their powers truly is. Unrestrained power is hazardous indeed. And those on the islands... I would expect they would know less of the truth as a result of being located so far from other wizards.

"For now," she continued, "you must rest and try to process all that you have learned today. It will not be easy. You will not find that sleep comes easy. When it comes, though, it will have healing power for your mind. Try not to discuss things between you, as that will just delay the healing sleep even longer."

Gisealia was glad for the soft and warm bed, it was

more luxurious than any she had ever experienced. Yet, just as Ree had said, it took a long time to settle her mind. She and Nikaijila whispered to each other in the dark a few times, but mostly they kept to their own thoughts. As she grew drowsy at last, Gisealia realized it was the first time since she had been taken from her family that she was allowed to fall asleep naturally.

She woke with a start the next morning, fearing that a supervisor would yell at her for sleeping late. She was briefly confused by the comfortable bed with no bunk over it, but her memory of the previous day quickly returned. She smiled at the ability to awaken naturally and not feel compelled to immediately get out of bed.

"What are you grinning about?" Nikaijila said with a smirk.

Gisealia looked over at her friend, who was already sitting up with her legs over the side of her bed.

"You know as well as I do," she said with a smile. "Normal sleep, what an incredible feeling."

"I'm glad to hear that you two are awake at last," Ree said from across the room. "I will have a solid breakfast for us soon, and then we must get to work."

Gisealia's expression turned thoughtful. "You have mentioned work several times, Ree, but you have not explained what work it is."

Ree gave a light laugh. "It is the work of teaching the two of you how to wield magic, so that we can begin the much bigger task of bringing an end to Eln-Ketaar."

"Now that," Nikaijila said, "is work I am eager to do."

"It will be dangerous work, when we oppose the wizards who profit from that evil place," Ree said. "I do not exaggerate when I say that you are probably being hunted at this very moment. I believe I can protect you here, because my home is so remote, and because I have carefully crafted spells to hide myself and my use of magic. When you leave my protection, though, you will be at risk. Your families will also be at risk, if the wizards use them as hostages. These are serious matters." She then laughed quietly again. "But we can have fun with your training, and I, too, am eager to free the women and girls trapped in Eln-Ketaar."

After their morning meal, the three women got right to work. Ree kept them busy all day, taking only brief breaks for rest and meals. When they went to bed the next night, both Gisealia and Nikaijila fell asleep quickly and slept soundly.

Although they spent many days with Ree, Gisealia did not have the same sense of losing time that she had experienced while imprisoned in Eln-Ketaar. She could see the sun, feel the weather, and watch one season slowly turn to another. She found Ree to be an effective mentor, but learning to control her power and draw power from around her was more difficult than she expected.

"First frost," Ree said one morning as she looked out a window at her garden. "We'd better finish harvesting the more sensitive vegetables today. And then, my sweet students, I think it is time to discuss your departure, for I think you have learned nearly all that I can teach you."

After their morning chores and after collecting from the garden what Ree wanted to protect from the frost, they took comfortable seats within her cottage and Ree served tea and sweet cakes again to go with their discussion.

"I have kept you busy since you arrived," the older woman said, "but I have been busy as well while you have been practicing. I have always kept an eye on Eln-Ketaar to be aware of events and changes there, but I also took the time to locate your families and have been watching them as well. I did not want any harm to come to them while I was training you here."

"Are they well?" Nikaijila spoke up.

"They are well, for now," Ree answered. "From what I have discerned, the risk is growing that they may be taken hostage to draw you out of hiding. The most powerful wizards are greatly disturbed that no trace of you has been seen since your sudden departure from Eln-Ketaar.

"There is another problem," she continued, "which does not arise from your escape but will concern you still. Indeed, it is something that could trouble all in the land, if the rumors are true. Far to the north, there is a powerful wizard named Volkellan. He has long had a reputation for dabbling with things he should not. In his advanced age, what little sanity and restraint he showed before may have disappeared. There is rumor... that he has summoned creatures that were long ago eradicated from the land."

"Creatures?" Gisealia asked.

"Dark and powerful beasts," Ree said. "Apparently, he thought it was... amusing. He saw each one as a challenge, and he took joy in solving each puzzle. He merely laughed at the destruction they caused. When he did this in the past, he would let them rampage a while before destroying them himself. Now... he has unleashed several, and there is rumor that Volkellan himself may have been killed by one."

Gisealia shook her head slowly. "Aside from presenting more danger, how does this affect us?"

"As much as the wizards of the land will not wish this to be the true," Ree said, "it is quite possible that they alone will not be able to stop all of these creatures. They are going to need help. And by help, I mean women who can wield magic."

Nikaijila raised her eyebrows. "You want us to fight *with* the men?"

Ree shrugged. "I want you to consider that it may be necessary whether you or they like it. First, we must release the women and girls in Eln-Ketaar, so that they can be trained. And to do that, we must defeat the men... only to turn around and join them to defeat the beasts."

"It sounds... futile," Gisealia commented.

"It may be," Ree said, her tone grim, "which will be a sad thing for all in the land, including your loved ones. We cannot guess at futility, though. We must do our best, and to do that, we must take on the most important task first. I believe that first important task is the protection of your families, which will allow you to focus on your next task. Future tasks are best left to the future."

Gisealia let out a quiet sigh. "So we must leave you, go to our homes, find a way to protect our families, and then..."

Ree smiled. "One step at a time, Gisealia. Yes, leaving is now appropriate, for there is little left for me to teach you. We can prepare for your departure as soon as you are ready. I think, for your safety, it will be best to travel together. Gisealia, your family is closer and easier to reach, so you should start there. Then, the two of you can go to Nikaijila's family."

Nikaijila turned up her palms in frustration. "But what are we to do with them? How do we protect them?"

"They need to be taken into hiding," Ree said calmly. "I can help with this, I can prepare temporary homes for them that should be nearly as safe as this cottage. Once in hiding, they must remain there until women are allowed to wield magic freely. Only then will there be no risk of your kin being used against you. You must go to them, though, and help them understand the need for this."

Gisealia nodded slowly. "I see the sense in this. We have become comfortable here, and we have enjoyed learning to use magic. Yet if our families are at risk, we must protect them. I will gladly turn from that task once completed and do whatever I can to end Eln-Ketaar. As for the beasts... that is too much to think about now."

"It is," Ree agreed, "but it is not something that should be forgotten. If you kill many wizards to free those in Eln-Ketaar, it may harm you later when you face those beasts."

"Kill..." Nikaijila said, her voice trailing away.

Ree nodded. "There will be violence ahead for both of you. I'm sorry to tell you this. Yet it started for you when you were taken from your homes. Now, it is time to return."

Gisealia sighed and looked down. "I agree," she said. "I will be sad to go, but it must be done."

"Will we see you again after we have gone?" Nikaijila asked.

"In person, it is hard to say, for we cannot know the future," Ree said. "We will see each other through magic, though, as I appeared to Gisealia in the mine.

We will need to coordinate our efforts to move your families to safety. Perhaps among those moves we will see each other in person too. Whether you will return here or not... it is hard to say."

Gisealia got to her feet. "Let us begin our preparations for our next journey," she said. "Now that the path is laid before us, I am eager to embark on it with little delay. Yet as I speak, I realize that I do not even know how to reach my family, for I do not know where we are. I have also little knowledge of my home village other than that it is on a lake in a forest among mountains. We will need guidance."

"You will need maps," Ree said with a grin as she stood up. "Come, Nikaijila. We will deal with today, today. Tomorrow will wait."

Chapter Five

"Are you sure we are not lost?" Nikaijila asked grumpily.

Gisealia laughed lightly. "Just because we accidentally slid down a hill on our backsides does not mean we are lost." She stood up and brushed the dirt from her clothes. "Come, the sun is already setting. We need to find a good place to camp for the night. Tomorrow, we should reach Seyelthe."

The younger woman stood and brushed herself off. "The beds in Eln-Ketaar were better than sleeping on the ground," she muttered.

"And how many nights have you said that since we left Ree's cottage?" Gisealia said with a smirk.

"Every single one," Nikaijila said. "Every. Single. One. I don't know why people ever settled in this land. It's cold, it's hard. Life on the island isn't like this."

"I look forward to seeing that for myself," Gisealia said with a grin.

"You doubt me?" her friend asked with exaggerated offense.

Gisealia laughed. "Not in the slightest! Come on, the day is wasting away."

The two young women set out through the forest again. They had mostly avoided the use of magic since they left the protection of Ree's cottage, although at times they used small spells to speed their travel, such as riding on the top of streams when the route of the water was a close enough match to the direction they wanted to travel.

When the forest became too dark to travel without a lantern or the use of magic for light, they settled into a protected nook created by a large log laying adjacent to a large boulder. With few words they ate a small amount of food and laid out the bedrolls that offered a bit of comfort in the wilderness.

They continued again the next morning as soon as it was light enough, since neither of them was comfortable or had slept well. Despite occasional attempts at humor or just light conversation, Gisealia knew that their moods were being dragged down by the trek across rugged terrain, the meager food, and the hazards they and their families faced. It seemed impossible to manage a grin more than briefly.

"We should be close," Gisealia said that afternoon. "I don't recognize it yet, but it feels right. What little of those far hills I could see through the trees looked about right."

"Let's take a short break," Nikaijila suggested. "We still have ample daylight. Just enough to rest our feet and have a little food."

Gisealia sighed, but she stopped anyway. "A short break." She looked around and spotted a log that seemed like a good place to sit. "Just enough to rest our feet a little and also eat," she said as she moved toward the log.

"I think I just said that," her friend said, smirking. Nikaijila then stopped. "I hear a stream nearby. A quick drink would also be nice."

"Fine, but be quick about it, and don't go too far," Gisealia said. "If it's echoing from a distance, just come back. We shouldn't become separated."

Nikaijila nodded. "I will come right back. Drink or no drink. I promise."

Gisealia watched her friend disappear through some brush. She felt uneasy being separated from

Nikaijila, but she tried to push away the feeling. She knew they had been nearly inseparable for many days, and she also knew that they would face serious risks and challenges once they reached Seyelthe. The anxiety was bound to bleed into other situations.

"Gisealia?" a male voice asked with obvious surprise.

She spun, knowing she recognized the voice but not immediately placing it. When she saw the white-haired old man walking toward her, it took her a moment to put a name to the face.

"Kanzlar," she said, her eyes wide.

Before she could do anything, he raised one hand and pointed at her. Gisealia saw nothing, but suddenly she felt like a heavy net had been thrown over her. She tried to draw in power from around her, but nothing happened. Fear raced through her mind as she realized that the old wizard was blocking her.

"You shouldn't be here!" he said as he stopped just out of reach. "I heard you escaped. I thought you would return here, but I expected you to arrive soon after your escape. I had just about given up on you coming back, but here you are. And back to Eln-Ketaar you will go!"

"No!" Gisealia snapped loudly, hoping that

Nikaijila would hear her. "I am not going back! You will never take me back there!"

Kanzlar shook his head. "Fool," he said. "Running away and putting everyone at risk. Even your family? You come back and expect them to allow you to stay? Think of your brother! How dare you endanger him with your presence? You disgust me."

"You disgust me," Gisealia snarled. "You know I'm not sick!"

"Oh, but you are," he scoffed. "You're very sick, and very dangerous. Yes, I know what that sickness is, but that doesn't make you any less dangerous. But enough talk. It is time to put you back where you belong, and this time you will find out what happens to the *worst* of the girls."

"No!" Gisealia screamed at him. "I will *not* go back there!"

Despite her words, she found herself standing up from the log against her will. Her arms snapped to her sides and she bowed her head, as her mind raged against his manipulation.

"I should make you kneel or crawl just for your disobedience and disrespect," Kanzlar sneered. "Only knowing what you will face when I bring you in, and knowing how richly they will reward me, keeps me from punishing you too severely now."

"Not going," she tried to reply, but he had taken control of her mouth. Her words were little more than grunts.

He chuckled. "Defiant to the end. Yes, my dear, you are going back to face your punishment in Eln-Ketaar."

"No, she's not," Nikaijila's voice came from nearby.

Kanzlar barely had time to look up before an invisible but powerful force knocked him off his feet. He cried out in pain and anger and tried to get up, but Nikaijila strode toward him in fury, raising one hand. Blue bolts of energy lanced out and struck at the wizard, again and again.

"Stop!" Gisealia finally cried out when she suddenly felt free again. "Stop! He's... he's dead."

"Come on!" Nikaijila cried out when she finally looked away from Kanzlar's body. "We have to go!"

She pulled on Gisealia's arm, but her friend kept staring down at the dead wizard she had known from her home village.

"Gisealia, we have to *leave*! Now!" Nikaijila pleaded. "That was a lot of magic. Someone will notice. They could appear at any moment! Please,

Gisealia. We have to run!"

Gisealia finally tore her eyes away from Kanzlar. "I..."

Her friend shook her head. "It doesn't matter. Run!"

This time when she pulled, Gisealia went with her. The two ran through the forest, heedless of the small branches and brush that slapped at their faces. Fear took over, and they ran with little more direction than getting as far as they could from the scene of Kanzlar's death.

"What do we do now?" Gisealia said when they finally slowed down.

Nikaijila shook her head slowly. "We keep going. We have a mission, we keep trying. We have to get to your family, now more than ever. We have to get them away, we have to get away ourselves, before one of the other wizards finds out that we killed that one."

"Kanzlar. His name was Kanzlar."

"I don't care what his name was," her friend said hotly. "He was trying to take you back. I wasn't going to let him do that. That's all that mattered then, it's all that matters now. Not his name."

Gisealia shrugged. "Sorry."

"Never mind," Nikaijila said after a moment. "We

just need to get to your family. Focus on that. Do you recognize anything yet? Can you get us there without the maps, or do we need to stop and figure out where we are?"

"I... I'm not sure."

"Well, keep looking. And get your mind clear, remember what Ree said. You have to control your mind, and right now it looks like you're not even trying."

Gisealia stopped short. "I *am* trying. I just... I've never killed anyone, I've never seen someone get killed. He... I... I never liked him, he was never friendly, but I still..."

Nikaijila turned and met her friend's gaze. "I'm sorry," she said with a sigh. "I'm terrified. I guess I shouldn't point fingers. I need to control my mind too."

"Thanks," Gisealia said softly after a moment. "I will try harder. Let's keep moving."

"Do you think we should contact Ree? Ask her advice?"

Gisealia shook her head. "No, I think we need to make our own decisions. I'm sure she would just say what you did, though, that we have our mission ahead of us and that we need to keep going."

They set out again through the forest, and Gisealia looked for every opportunity to see through the trees toward the hills she had noticed before. They had looked familiar but at the same time not entirely so, as if they were at the wrong angle. When she did catch another glimpse of them, she paused a moment to stare and then caught up with her friend.

"I think we need to veer to the left," she said. "I just looked at those hills again. I have a good idea where we are, but we're slightly off track."

"Left it is," Nikaijila said.

They tried to be quiet and listen for other people as they moved through the forest, but they had limited success. There were many leaves and branches on the ground, and the underbrush was often thick. With no trail to follow, they often found themselves plunging blindly into something and forcing their way through, which they couldn't do quietly.

After going through a particularly difficult patch of brush, they stopped to rest briefly. They said nothing, having lost any desire to chat idly or make small jokes. After catching their breath, Gisealia gestured for them to continue, and her friend gave a short nod. A moment later, they both stopped as an odd sound reached their ears.

"Was that... a large bird?" Nikaijila asked in a whisper.

Gisealia shook her head. "Too slow, it sounded wrong for a bird. Maybe... maybe it was just a strange wind in the tops of the trees."

Her friend raised her eyebrows. "A rhythmic wind?"

"I don't know," Gisealia said with a shrug. "Whatever it is, it's gone. Let's go."

Not long after their short break, Gisealia saw a large rotten stump that she recognized, although it had broken down much more since she last saw it. She quickly stopped and reached out to grab Nikaijila's arm.

"We're here," she said softly. "Seyelthe is just over there." She pointed through the forest. "I know where I am now. I'll lead the way, I can get us on a trail that will take us almost directly to my family's cottage."

They had only taken a few steps when they heard the sound again, and this time it was louder. A dark shadow passed over the forest near them.

"What is that?" Nikaijila said, her voice full of fear.

"I don't know, but it can't be good," Gisealia said. "Let's run!"

She took the lead, darting through the trees, with her friend at her heels. When she found the trail she wanted, she turned sharply onto it and sprinted toward the village. Her mind raced with possibilities and fears when the first buildings came into view.

A scream from the village ahead of them wiped away Gisealia's other thoughts.

"Dragon!" a woman's voice cried out. "There's a dragon!"

Gisealia and Nikaijila exchanged terrified glances, but they didn't stop. More shouts of fear arose from the village as they approached. When they broke out into the open, both of them looked to the sky. They could see nothing, but there was no doubt in Gisealia's mind that a dragon had found Seyelthe.

"One of Volkellan's beasts?" Nikaijila yelled as she followed Gisealia into the village.

"A reasonable guess!" Gisealia answered hurriedly. "Here! This is my family's cottage!"

She ran toward the door, but before she could reach it, the door opened to reveal a young man holding a bow with an arrow nocked. It took her a moment to realize she was looking at her brother.

Gonterill stopped in the doorway, staring at the two young women rushing toward his home. Cries of fear and shouts for weapons filled the air, and a shadow swept over Gisealia and Nikaijila.

"Gonterill!" Gisealia said.

"Who are you?" he demanded.

"It's Gisealia! Your sister!" she answered.

He shook his head. "Get away! My sister is gone. I don't know who you are, but get away from me! This is no time for pranks, there is a *dragon* to fight!"

"Your sister came back," Nikaijila spoke up. "This truly is Gisealia, I can vouch for her."

Gonterill looked at her with a disturbed expression. "I don't know you either. What *are* you?"

"Gonterill!" Gisealia snapped. "What a thing to ask a person you just met! She's a young woman just like me!"

He shook his head. "What's wrong with her skin? What happened to her?"

Nikaijila snickered, but Gisealia was incensed. "Nothing *happened* to her, and there's nothing *wrong* with her skin! It's just a different color! And why are we even—"

"Gisealia?" a man's voice caught her attention from one side. "Is that you?"

She looked over to see her old neighbor, also holding a bow with an arrow nocked but staring at her in shock.

"It is me, Teslarkin," she confirmed. "Please vouch for me to my fool of a brother."

Teslarkin scanned the sky and then looked back at her. "Are you cured?"

"I... in a sense," she said with a shrug. "It's a long story that must wait!"

"Yes, please, let's wait!" Nikaijila said urgently. "There's a dragon on the loose!"

Gisealia turned to her brother. "Where is father? He should be out here–"

Her words were cut off by a loud roar followed by screams. Their gazes snapped toward the center of the village where they saw the dragon rising into the air with flames springing up underneath it. Gonterill hastily pushed past the two young women in front of his cottage.

"I don't know who you are," he said over his shoulder, "but my father died last year."

"He..." Gisealia's voice faltered, and she felt faint.

Nikaijila tore her eyes away from watching the dragon arc above the lake. She grasped one of Gisealia's arms and pulled her friend close.

"Gisealia! Gisealia! I'm sorry, I'm very sorry for the loss of your father, but... let's kill a dragon today! We will grieve your father's passing in due time. Right now there's a dragon to hunt! Let us prove that women can and *should* wield magic. Let the bowmen waste their arrows, that dragon is ours! There's no time to waste, it's coming back!"

"Magic?" Teslarkin asked as he aimed his bow skyward. "Did you say magic?"

"You!" Nikaijila snapped, pointing at him. "Be quiet!"

Teslarkin's face registered surprise at being spoken to that way, but he kept his face to the sky.

"It's time, Gisealia!" her friend urged. "Let us take this beast down!"

Without waiting for agreement, Nikaijila turned and pointed at the dragon that was now swooping down on the village. She released a flurry of energy bolts that slammed into its side as arrows from the villagers fell short. The dragon swung its head toward her and let out a deafening bellow.

"Gisealia! Now!"

Nikaijila let out another flurry of bolts at the dragon's face as it raced toward them. It was nearly there when Gisealia looked up. She held up one hand

and launched a dense wall of air at the beast. Fire appeared in the dragon's mouth just before the blast hit. The flames sprayed harmlessly back around the dragon's body as it faltered and banked toward the lake again.

"Not quite what I would have chosen," Nikaijila remarked.

"You wanted to be caught in its flames?" Gisealia shot back.

"You knew before it breathed that fire that it was going to do so?" her friend challenged her as they watch the beast turn itself around over the water.

"Oh, be silent and focus on killing this thing before it destroys more of my village," Gisealia growled.

"Kill it, now that is clever," Nikaijila said with a smirk. "I should have thought of that myself."

The two fell silent and prepared their magic for the next assault. This time when the dragon came back at the village, it was clearly aiming directly for them. While it was still over the water, both of them unleashed a torrent of bolts of energy that slammed into its face, wings, and body. Still, the dragon came at them.

"This isn't working," Gisealia said tersely as she

fought back panic. More arrows went up from the village, but they had less effect than the magic. "This isn't working!"

"Get ready to deflect its flames again!" Nikaijila snapped as she released more bolts of energy.

In the corner of her eye, Gisealia saw her brother aiming at the oncoming dragon. With sudden inspiration, she stopped her attack on the dragon.

"Gisealia?" her friend said, sounding alarmed.

Gisealia didn't answer. She watched and waited for Gonterill to release his arrow. As soon as it was in the air, she poured magic into it and sped it through the air.

With the magic flowing freely through her, time seemed to slow. She knew her friend was yelling at her, but she focused on the precise flight of the arrow. She streamed her powers into it, hardening it and guiding it at the same time. It sank so deep into the dragon's body that it disappeared entirely. Gisealia then triggered the last magic effect by making the arrowhead explode into tiny, white-hot bits.

Nikaijila's terrified screams were drowned out by the shriek of the dragon as it passed low over their heads. A moment later, it plowed into the trees of the forest beyond the village, breaking through thick trunks as if they were twigs. The beast's body hit the ground hard enough that Gisealia felt it through her feet.

"Is it gone?" Nikaijila asked in wonder when the cacophony ended. "Is it dead?"

Gisealia nodded slowly as she started to tremble. "It's gone. It's dead."

Nikaijila grabbed her into a tight hug. "I thought *we* were going to be dead."

"Not yet," Gisealia said. "Not yet." She gently pushed her friend back to look her in the eye. "Contact Ree. Tell her what happened. Tell her people saw us fighting the dragon. I must talk to Gonterill now and find my mother. We need to get ourselves away from here. We need to get my family... what remains of my family away from Seyelthe.

"The wizards in Eln-Ketaar surely detected this," she continued grimly. "We must move fast, but we can succeed. We will succeed! We will get my family to safety, and your family will be next. One thing at a time, as Ree said. Will you contact her and ask for her help to get my kin away before the wizards arrive?"

Nikaijila gave a quick nod. "I will do that now." She looked past Gisealia for a moment. "Go. Your handsome brother is waiting to talk to you."

"Handsome?" Gisealia asked sharply, raising an eyebrow as her friend moved away.

"*We must move fast*, Gisealia," her friend said, looking back and giving her a quick wink. "Go!"

A Note From Stuart

Although set in a world with magic and monsters, this novella was inspired by a true story in our world, many years ago. The real story did not have a happy ending. Instead of being blessed with magic, the "main character" in real life was afflicted with what was apparently cerebral palsy.

At least half of my earnings from this book will be donated toward cerebral palsy research and/or patient care.

Cerebral palsy is very common. In the time it took you to read The Secret of Eln-Ketaar, many new babies were born with it. I encourage you to familiarize yourself with cerebral palsy—what we know about its potential causes and risk factors, the forms it can take, and the impact it has on those who have it and their families & caretakers. If possible, I also encourage you to consider donating to a suitable organization that seeks to improve the lives of those with cerebral palsy and/or prevent it in the future.

Thank you for taking the time to read this story and to consider how you might positively impact those affected by cerebral palsy.

If you enjoyed The Secret of Eln-Ketaar, please mention it to a friend!

More From
Stuart J. Whitmore

Honest reviews are always appreciated! You can read more of my short fiction, for free, in the *Distant Worlds* sampler. It is exclusively available as a bonus for subscribing to my newsletter. You can find a link to do that, along with information about my other books, on my site:

StuartWhitmoreAuthor.com

Other titles include:

The Vengeance of Mirickar
The Ambitions of Kreltahk
The Wanderings of Joramm

Journey to Yandol, and other stories
KINRU
No Fanfare

Two Boys, Two Planets

Acknowledgments

First and foremost, I must thank my father, for if he had not shared with me some family history, this story would have never been written.

Thanks also go to Jacob and Brandy, for their inspiration to finish writing and publishing this novella when things turned bad for me personally and I was tempted to give up on it.

Many thanks go to Mickenzie for her patience, support, encouragement, and inspiration during the writing of this tale. My appreciation for her goes far beyond this novella.

I cannot neglect to thank Holly and Jared for their edits and suggestions which saved this novella from suffering from distractions that escaped my attention.

Finally, unending thanks go to Jeff for being a steadfast friend throughout many difficult years. There are many other books that would never have been completed without his support.

www.ingramcontent.com/pod-product-compliance
Lightning Source LLC
Chambersburg PA
CBHW020633130626
46552CB00003B/1198